ECHOES OF THE SILENT HEART

Written by Mr. Avinash

Nonia Books

Published by Nonia Books

Paperback ISBN: 978-93-344-2645-8

Acknowledgement

There was a time when I found myself in a very dark place, caught between silence and pain, unsure if I could ever step out of it. Writing these stories became a way for me to confront that struggle, to give shape to feelings I could not voice, and to begin finding a path forward.

This collection was born out of that experience. My hope is that those who read these pages may find some reflection of their own struggles, and perhaps a small sense of comfort in knowing they are not alone. If these stories can help even a little in the process of carrying grief, surviving silence, or remembering love, then they will have done what I intended.

Contents

Story 1: Scars of Sindoor 1

Story 2: Rosa 10

Story 3: A Mother's Cry 19

Story 4: Behind the Smile 25

Story 5: Lipstick in Red Light 35

Story 6: The Night of the Unspoken Battles 40

Story 7: Till the Last Flame Lasts 46

Author's Note 54

STORY 1

Scars of Sindoor

I crouched on the edge of the stone path, scattering crumbs from my hand to a scruffy brown dog. Its tail thumped against the rocks in a clumsy rhythm, and I laughed quietly as it snapped up each piece. The morning sun spilled over the jagged peaks of Kashmir, turning the valley into a wash of gold and rose. The crisp air smelled of pine and distant tea stalls, sharp and sweet. From below, I could hear the faint hum of vehicles on the winding roads, mingling with the cheerful chirping of birds.

Our group had stopped in a wide open field, where a few tents had been set up to shelter us for breakfast. Children's ran between them, laughter ringing out, while adults poured tea and shared small stories. The warm sun touched my skin, and the breeze carried the faint smell of wet grass and flowers.

"Careful, feed it too much and it'll start following you home," Raj teased, a fellow traveller in our group, lifting his cup of tea as he laughed. Across the table, a Sikh couple guided their young son as he balanced a cup of tea in his hands. The mother's gold bangle caught the sunlight as she gently steadied him, and I smiled at their quiet joy. Everyone in our little group came from different corners of India, different faiths, different languages. Here, we shared laughter, tea, and the thrill of being alive.

I felt Arjun's presence before I saw him. He stepped up beside me, brushing a strand of hair from my face. "Hey," he whispered, and before I could react, he kissed me. His lips were gentle and full of the quiet promise of safety.

I giggled, stepping back. "Not here... people are watching." My cheeks burned.

He grinned. “I’m in the army; I can claim my bride wherever I want.” His eyes twinkled with mischief, but there was that underlying reassurance, a promise to always protect and always be nearby. I wanted this moment to stretch forever, the soft sunlight on his face, the smell of pine, the faint taste of tea on my lips.

I reached up, almost self-consciously, to adjust the line of sindoor in my hair. It still felt strange and new, its deep red a reminder of vows barely weeks old. Arjun’s eyes softened as he noticed the gesture, and he murmured, “It suits you.”

And then the first shot rang out.

It tore through the morning like a blade, splitting the air, shattering birdsong and laughter alike. At first, I didn’t understand, but a cold shiver ran down from my spine. The dog yelped and darted into the nearby trees.

Then movement from the trees caught my attention. Figures stepped out, rifles glinting in the sunlight. My mind struggled to process— who were they? Why were they here? Panic surged, cold and sharp. People around me began to scream, scrambling to gather their children, clutching cups and plates, trying to make sense of the sudden terror.

I clung to Arjun, my fingers digging into his jacket.

“Hide under the table” Raj shouted, but it offered almost no cover. The tent was open on all sides; a flimsy canvas stretched over poles. There was nowhere to run.

The attackers moved with purpose, sweeping the field, eyes scanning every corner, rifles ready.

My chest tightened and I could hear my own heartbeat thundering in my ears. And then they began rounding people up, dragging them toward the center of the field. Then a gunman came near our tent with his rifle gleaming in the sunlight. He pointed his gun to us and commanded us to move to the center of the field. We heard his voice, but my legs refused to move with fear. He barked orders again, but this time Arjun's hand found mine, gripping tightly, and I forced myself to follow him, trembling, every step slow and heavy.

Around us, others were being pushed and shoved, crying, pleading, moving in a tense, chaotic line toward the center. The open field stretched before us, offering no cover. The tents we had sheltered under felt like fragile paper against the violence closing in. Children clutched their parents, faces pale and eyes wide, while the adults tried to steady them, murmuring reassurances that sounded hollow even to themselves.

Step by step, we moved toward the center of the field, the distance seeming endless. Every movement felt measured, deliberate, as if time itself had slowed. After a short while we reached the center, where they pressed us together with the other families, a cluster of terrified bodies. Each face told its own story of confusion and fear. I clutched Arjun's jacket, seeking some fragment of safety in the midst of chaos, my fingers trembling.

Then the attackers began their methodical separation, one of them shouted an order and pointed to a man. He was dragged forward as his wife clung to him, pleading, but they shoved her aside. I remembered him. His name was Mahesh, and he had offered us parathas that morning when he noticed our plate was empty. I had seen him laugh with his daughter when she spilled pickle on her dress, wiping it away with a father's patience. Now he was forced forward, the gunman demanding he recite the Kalma, the Islamic declaration of faith. His lips trembled as he whispered that he did not know the words. The rifle cracked and he dropped lifeless to the dirt. His wife wailed, her cries cutting through the valley like a knife.

Then another was dragged out, struggling as his old mother tried to hold him back. I knew him too. Joseph. He had been soft spoken, serving his mother tea at breakfast before anyone else. I remembered how carefully he had tucked her shawl around her shoulders in the chill of the morning. Now his voice shook as they ordered him to recite. He shook his head. A gunshot. His body jerked and fell. His mother sank to the ground, rocking his body in her lap as if he were a child again, whispering words no one could hear.

And then they came for us. Rough hands tore Arjun

from my side. I clung to him desperately, nails digging into his arm, begging them not to take him. One of the men kicked me hard and I fell to the ground. Arjun tried to resist, but a rifle was jammed beneath his chin and he froze. They dragged him to the front, pushing him into the same place where the others had fallen.

The world spun around me, soundless and heavy. My thoughts blurred. Only moments ago, he had been beside me, his shoulder brushing mine, his warmth steady against the morning chill. Now he stood alone, facing death.

Memories surged, tripping over each other in a flood. It had been only weeks since our wedding, the colors of that day still vivid in my mind. He had fought for this short leave from the army, pleading again and again until they finally gave him a handful of days. He told me it was worth every salute, every request, every weary wait in dusty offices, just to be here with me.

We had dreamed of this trip like children whispering about stolen sweets. He had promised me snow, though it was not the season. He said he would show me mountains that looked as if they touched heaven. He had promised photographs, me standing in front of the pines, him pretending to look serious but failing every time because he could never hold back his grin when I was near. He had promised stories, evenings by a fire where we would plan a future so wide and bright it could not possibly fit inside the walls of our small rented house.

I had believed him. I had built castles of thought around his promises. I saw myself waking every morning to his voice, the weight of his arm draped across me, the smell of tea on the stove mixing with the starch of his uniform. I saw myself learning the rhythm of a soldier's life, waiting for his return, writing letters that carried not just words but my breath, my longing, my entire world folded into pages.

I had dreamed of the children we might have, his steady eyes, my restless laughter. I had dreamed of holidays filled with noisy relatives, of summers when he would chase our son across the courtyard, of winters when he would wrap a shawl around my shoulders and scold me for never dressing warmly enough. I had dreamed of grey hair and wrinkled hands, of sitting side by side watching the world grow smaller, knowing that every piece of it we had endured together.

And now all those dreams wavered before me like fragile glass, trembling, ready to shatter.

My mehendi had not yet faded. My hands still smelled of a new beginning, of the life we had just stepped into. Only yesterday, when I traced the fading patterns, I had wondered how long they would last, how long before they disappeared into skin and memory.

And then the gun cracked.
The sound tore the air apart.

I could not breathe. My chest refused to rise. My

mind screamed, but my body sat frozen, useless, as if it too had surrendered. Arjun's body crumpled, collapsing like a puppet whose strings had been cut, the dust rising around him in a small, cruel cloud.

I stared. My mind was blank, a white sheet that no thought could stain.

The man I had married, the man I had loved, the man who had promised me a lifetime had fallen into the dirt like he had never belonged to it at all.

My body moved before my mind could make any sense. Somehow, I dragged myself across the dirt to where he had fallen. My arms trembled as I lifted his head and placed it in my lap, rocking him as if he might wake. His blood soaked into my clothes, warm at first and then chilling against my skin. I wailed until my throat was raw, until my voice broke into nothing. Time unraveled around me. I could not tell if minutes or hours had passed. The screams, the gunshots, the chaos of the world blurred into silence. All I knew was the stillness of his body, the unbearable weight of his head in my lap.

When at last the gunmen vanished and the field fell into a hollow quiet, I remained where I was, motionless. I did not know if others had survived, or if the sun had crossed to the other side of the mountains. It was only when a policewoman's shadow fell over me that I stirred. She knelt and asked softly if I was alright. I wanted to answer, wanted to cry, but no sound came. My tears had already dried, leaving nothing but a hollow ache where grief should have been. My hand drifted to my forehead without thinking, and I felt only dust and sweat where my sindoor had once been.

****

STORY 2

Rosa

They call me black as though the word itself were poison, something to spit out quickly before it burns the tongue. The children shout it with cruel delight, the elders mutter it like a warning, and together their voices turn my feathers into a mark of shame.

Black. Unlucky. Cursed.

I have heard it so many times that the sound clings to me more tightly than the wind clings to my wings.

When I descend to the square, their hatred always waits. Sometimes it comes as stones that slice the air before they slice at me; sometimes as sticks swung by boys who run after me, laughing as though torment were a sport. I twist and rise until the rooftops shrink below me, and only then do I escape. Up in the sky the world forgets what I am. Up there, in the clean breath of the wind, I am nothing but movement and freedom.

But freedom is fragile thing. Hunger always finds me. It drags me back down, forcing me into the square where the curses live, where the stones wait, where my shadow is unwelcome.

The square does not belong to me. It belongs to the pigeons.

They walk proudly across the stones, pale-gray feathers flashing whenever the sun strikes them. Their cooing is met with laughter, their fluttering with clapping hands. Children scatter grain before them as though giving tribute to little kings. Old women lower their palms with smiles, and the pigeons gather without fear, without hesitation. They are considered gentle, harmless, even holy.

I watch from the edges, never daring to come close. I am the thief, the shadow, the bird that brings misfortune. For the pigeons, abundance; for me, suspicion. No one throws stones at them. No one hisses them away.

Sometimes, I wonder if I was born wearing the wrong feathers. If the accident of color had been kinder, would the world's hands have opened to me as well? Would children's voices have called me pretty instead of cursed? Would I still be chased, still be hunted, still be despised?

But feathers do not change, and curses do not fade. So, I circle high, waiting for scraps the pigeons leave behind.

A grain. A crust.

A mercy too small for them to notice.

Once, long ago, I tried to join them. I slipped into their circle, pretending I was just another bird pecking at crumbs. For a heartbeat no one noticed. My beak touched a kernel of corn, sweet and golden. But before I could swallow, a hand swept down. Fingers clamped around my neck and the world tilted into terror. The boy who caught me shouted, his friends cheering as I thrashed. My wings beat uselessly, as his nails kept scraping my feathers. I felt like nothing more than a rag, a joke, a shadow that had dared to step into the light.

I never learned what he planned to do. In desperation I jabbed my beak into his palm. He cried out, his grip loosening, and I tore free into the sky, my heart pounding, his laughter chasing me into the clouds.

I did not return to the circle after that. Hunger might press me, but pride kept me at the edges. The pigeons were welcome, and I was not.

Still, hunger never forgets. It whispers louder than fear, more insistent than memory. It presses me down again and again, no matter how many times the stones rise to meet me.

There is one boy whose face I know too well. Hair the color of dust, a grin always ready. He carries stones in his pockets as though they are coins meant only to be spent on me. I know the sound of his breath before he throws. I know the sting when the pebble catches my wing. He grins when I flinch.

Others join him sometimes, a whole gang running with sticks and laughter, their shouts sharp with triumph. They chase me in circles until I break free. To them it is only a game. To me it is survival.

They have their pigeons to adore, yet still they crave me to despise. It is not enough to love what is pale and plump; something dark must be punished beside it.

I fly higher, higher, until the square shrinks and the

people below become specks. The sky cradles me, forgiving and endless. But the sky does not feed me.

My belly twists until every beat of my wings feels like a wound. My beak aches with longing, not for delicacies, but for anything at all: a seed, a crust, a careless crumb. The pigeons never know this. They have plenty to eat, always offered without thought. Sometimes I wonder if they even understand what hunger is.

I drift to the edges of the city, searching. The fields beyond are bare this season. The gutters hold nothing but ash. Even the rubbish heaps are picked clean. Each landing brings only disappointment. Each moment makes me weaker.

One evening as I find myself perched on a cracked wall, panting. A group of pigeons flies overhead, their full bellies reflected in their soft cooing I feel myself shrinking against the stone beneath me, and I wonder how much longer I can bear it.

It is then I hear a voice. Not sharp with cruelty, not edged with scorn, but soft, almost tuneless, carrying through the air like a thread of strange music.

I look down and see a girl sitting on the edge of the fountain, with a small bundle of cloth beside her. Her head tilts slightly, as if listening to something only she can sense. Her gaze is gentle yet blind to the bustle around her.

She scatters crumbs with careful fingers and the pigeons rush to them immediately. As their wings brush against her knees, she does not flinch. Instead, she smiles faintly. Her hand lowers again, dropping another few pieces, not to any bird in particular, but as though to the ground itself, to anyone who might be hungry.

I hesitate, convinced this must be a trick. Yet her movements are too calm, too deliberate, too gentle to be false.

I hover for a long moment, torn between caution and need. But my hunger wins at last. I descend, landing a few feet away. The pigeons glare at me, puffing their feathers, but the girl tilts her head as though hearing me arrive.

Her hand opens, and a crumb rests delicately in her palm.

Every instinct tells me to flee. I remember the boy's grip around my throat, the taunts, the stones. My claws scrape against the stone. But her hand does not move. She waits patiently.

A pigeon beats me to it, pecking her palm, scattering the crumb. She laughs softly, not angry, just amused. "Greedy little things," she murmurs.

The sound of her voice startles me. No venom, no disdain. Just lightness.

Before fear can take me, I dart forward, my beak snapping up a fragment of the scattered crumb. My heart hammers as I brace for the blow, the shout, the strike.

But nothing comes.
Only her hand, steady. Only her smile.
For the first time, I eat without being chased.
I return the next day. And the next.

She is always there, scattering crumbs, humming, sitting in her silence. At first, I linger on the edge, only daring to snatch what falls. Then I perch closer. One morning my feathers brush her hand as I reach for the grain. She laughs softly, as she always does.

She tilts her head, listening to the flap of my wings. "You are not like the others," she murmurs. "You need a name that is yours. Rosa. Yes, Rosa." The word wraps around me gently, like a small light in the darkness. Rosa. For the first time, I am something more than the black feathers the world despises.

The pigeons still crowd her, but I have a place too now.

Something inside me begins to change. The old words still haunt me: unlucky, cursed. But when I am near her, they seem less certain. In her presence, I feel neither thief nor shadow. I feel seen.

I almost forget the meaning of hunger.

Until the day it ends.

It is a late afternoon and the square is filled with restless footsteps and voices. She rises from the fountain, lifting her basket into her arms. Her cane taps steadily as she steps forward, her face lifted toward the sun. She moves with a calm that makes me believe she is safe.

I follow from above, gliding in slow circles.

The sound erupts suddenly. A roar of harsh grinding of wheels against the stone path. A cart— no, not a cart, faster than a cart, races through the square. Startled, pigeons burst into the sky as shouts erupt all around.

The girl does not turn her head. She cannot see it.

Someone cries for her to move, but she does not move.

The world narrows around me, every detail sharpening and twisting until nothing exists but the girl and the threat hurtling toward her. My wings pump with desperate speed, beating against the wind as though I could tear a path through it. My voice bursts out in a raw, piercing scream that shreds the air, a sound meant to warn, to plead, to stop what is coming. But no one hears me. No one reaches her in time.

The impact hits with a brutality that steals the breath from my wings. A heavy, crushing thud shakes the stones beneath her, and she collapses, her small body folding against the hard ground. The basket she carries tips over, spilling crumbs in a careless arc across the square, glittering faintly in the fading sunlight.

For a single heartbeat the world seems to hold its breath, silence pressing against my every wingbeat. Then the square explodes into chaos as shouts tear the air, feet pound the stones, and hands wave in panic. But it is too late, far too late to stop what has already happened.

My raw and desperate cries shatter the sky as the pigeons flee in panic, leaving the grain scattered and forgotten.

And there, on the cold stones, rests the only voice that ever called me something other than cursed, silenced and broken.

I circle above, with raw and desperate cries, but no one hears.

She is gone.
And I remain.

They call me black, they call me cursed. And at last, I believe them.

****

STORY 3

A Mother's Cry

The courthouse looms before me like a stone coffin with windows. I have walked this street before, but today each step feels heavier, as though the ground itself is aware of what I carry. The doors rise ahead in their weight of polished wood and metal, reflecting a sky that feels too bright for what must take place inside.

I pause for a moment at the threshold, and think of how many mothers have walked through doors like these, forced to sit and listen as men in suits turn the lives of their children into evidence and argument.

At the security gate I find a familiar face. My neighbor stands there in his crisp uniform, but his eyes betray what his mouth will not say. He looks at me with the faintest hesitation, as though he has always known this day would come, and when his hand lifts toward the scanner then falls away, I realize he has made a choice. Without a word he steps aside and lets me pass, the silence between us heavier than any command. The gesture feels like a confession, as if he too believes justice cannot live inside these walls. I clutch my coat closer and move forward, the weight hidden beneath it pressing steady against my ribs.

The air inside the courtroom feels different, thinner somehow, as if even the walls are reluctant to breathe. The benches stretch out in ordered rows, their wood worn smooth by years of restless bodies, and already they are filled with people who lean toward one another in anxious silence. Their voices move softly but persistently, a murmur that creeps through the stillness like the restless hum of insects at night. I walk to the back, lower myself onto a bench, and fold my hands in my lap, but nothing inside me is still enough to rest.

And then my eyes find him.

Heinrich sits at the front with his shoulders lowered and his hands neatly folded, his hair trimmed and his shirt pressed as though he were waiting for something ordinary, a simple errand to conclude. That plainness is what sickens me most. Evil should have horns or scars or the twisted face of nightmare, but instead it wears the mask of an ordinary man. It is that ordinariness that destroyed Alena.

The world around me begins to blur, the benches and robes fading into dull shades of gray, until all I can see is her. I see her in those last hours, her small hands clenching in terror, her voice breaking into a cry that tore itself raw from her throat, her body trembling under the shadow of the man who now sits only a few feet away.

Mama, she must have called, though no one came. Mama.

Each time I imagine it, the wounds open again.

The prosecutor's voice drags me back to reality. His words fall in steady rhythm, polished by practice, each one landing with the weight of a stone— abduction, violation, murder. They are words I have heard too many times, yet each one still cuts as though spoken for the first time. Every syllable seems carved into me, each detail echoing the story I already live inside.

Then the defense rises. His lawyer talks of Heinrich as though he were the real victim, as though the cruelty of his own past might somehow diminish the cruelty of his act. He asks us to see him as broken, shaped by pain, deserving of pity. Heinrich bows his head and tilts his face down as if in shame, but I see the faint flicker at the corner of his mouth, the half-formed smile he cannot quite hide. He is not ashamed. He is remembering. *He still carries her in him, as though Alena belongs to him.*

My nails press so hard into my palms that blood rises in thin crescents, but I keep my eyes fixed on him. I imagine rising now, crossing the room, and closing my hands around his throat until his breath fails him. For a moment I almost believe I can feel the strength of it, his pulse fading beneath my fingers. But I know my hands alone are not enough. That is why I have brought what lies hidden beneath my coat, waiting cool and certain for its use.

I close my eyes and summon Alena back, not broken now but whole. I see her in the kitchen, swinging her legs beneath the chair while brushing crumbs from her lap as laughter spills out of her mouth. I see her curled beside me at night, whispering half-formed stories until sleep gently carries her away. I see her in the garden, her arms lifted as she chases butterflies that always danced just beyond her grasp. These are the fragments I have clung to, but each day they fade further, like photographs left too long beneath the sun. He stole them from me, piece by piece, until almost nothing remained.

The rhythm of the courtroom recedes into a dull hum. Voices fall away into a blur of empty ritual, words spinning like leaves I cannot hear. What I hear instead is my own heartbeat, loud and unyielding, filling the hollow spaces of my body. With every thud I feel her voice calling me back, faint but insistent, pulling me toward the moment I can no longer resist.

I rise from the bench and the creak of the wood seems to cut through the room like a cry. Heads turn toward me, whispers faltering into silence as my steps carry me forward. I do not falter, because it feels as though the ground itself is guiding me, drawing me toward the place where everything will end.

My hand finds its way into my coat, and the metal is there, cold yet strangely familiar, as though it has always been meant for my palm. When I draw it out, time itself seems to pause. The people around me are frozen in their seats, their mouths half-formed into gasps that never quite sound. Even the dust in the beam of light above hangs suspended, as though the air refuses to move.

Heinrich lifts his head at last, and his eyes meet mine. For the first time there is no disguise. I see surprise break across his face, then confusion, and finally the flicker of fear. He understands.

I raise the gun, my finger curling around the trigger as though it has waited years for this moment. My breath steadies. My vision sharpens. In the silence I hear her laughter again, bright and unbroken, rising above the weight of everything that has drowned me.

I pull the trigger.

The first shot cracks the air like thunder, tearing apart the silence. His body jerks forward and his mask of composure ripped away in an instant. Gasps erupt behind me, but I do not hear them clearly. I fire again, and again, until the rhythm of the shots and the pounding of my heart blur into one relentless beat.

When the gun falls silent, he is slumped against the table, his head bowed one final time. The faint curl of his mouth is gone.

Chaos erupts around me. People scream, benches scrape against the floor, bodies scatter in every direction, but inside me there is only stillness. Smoke curls lazily through the air, its sharp scent filling my lungs, and beneath it all I hear the sound I thought I had lost forever.

Alena's laughter. Alena's voice. Alena's life.

Someone lowered my gun. My arm trembles, not only from the shot but from the release of months of grief, months of rage that no court could contain. I know the cost that will follow, but it does not matter. The weight that has crushed me for so long has lifted, leaving behind only the ache of something finished at last.

"This is for my little angel. For Alena."

****

STORY 4

Behind the Smile

The applause cracks through the ballroom like gunfire. My body wants to duck, and to reach for a weapon that is not even there. Yet I lock my knees and force my hands to stay at my sides. The sound rolls on relentlessly, pressing against me until I cannot tell if it is celebration or an attack.

I blink into the camera lights which burn hot and white. The crowd beyond seems like a haze of shapes, clapping in a rhythm. The sound of their celebration swells until it becomes nothing but noise.

The words echo in my head: "*Stay steady. Do not flinch. Do not let them see.*"

The medal rests heavy against my chest, silver and heavy, and I feel its weight not just on my uniform but on the memories that cling to it. The nights I cannot name, on the moments that replay in fragments behind my eyes like fire and and steel tearing the world apart. Fingers reach for my hand as I step down from the stage, strangers pressing close with smiles and congratulations. Their touch feels like sparks on my skin. I smile back because that is what they came for, because that is what is expected.

"*Smile. Nod. Shake their hands. Make them believe.*"

The voices follow me into every handshake and every camera flash. The cameras blink like muzzle fire, bursts that trigger something inside me. I see the mouths of reporters moving, only to catch fragments like hero, sacrifice, proud nation, but the words smear together before they land.

"*Answer if you must. Keep it simple. Keep it clean.*"

I feel the medal shift with every movement, dragging me backward. Not to the ballroom, not to this room of polished shoes and pressed suits, but to places where the air was full of sand and smoke, where the sky cracked open with fire and the ground shook with steel. My chest tightens as if it remembers before I do. My jaw aches from the smile I cannot let slip.

And then I see them.

My wife stands slightly apart from the cluster of cameras and reporters; her eyes fixed on me as if I might shatter. Our two kids cling to her, one small hand around her wrist, and the other clutching the hem of her dress. Their eyes shine with something between pride and fear.

"Stand tall. Do not let them see what is left of you."

I move to them because my legs know where to go even if the rest of me does not. My daughter throws her arms around me, pressing her small heartbeat against the medal. Meanwhile, my son watches, his hand half raised as if he is not sure if he can reach me.

"Smile for them. Do not let them know you are already gone."

The cameras click louder when my family is close. They mean nothing against the pounding of my own heart, against the memories that press forward like smoke through a door left open. I hold my smile, careful and practiced, and wonder how long it will last once the applause fades, once the flashes die, once the crowd leaves and I am left with the quiet that knows the truth.

"Keep breathing. Keep smiling. They cannot know."

A man in a well-tailored suit steps forward and shakes my hand, firm and practiced. Cameras tilted toward us, flashes marking the moment. Every movement feels rehearsed for everyone but me. My fingers itch to grip, to strike, to defend.

"Keep it steady. Do not betray it," I tell myself.

I smile and nod, because that is what they want to see, what my wife wants to see, what the world expects. Behind my eyes, sand and smoke rise. I hear voices screaming over the roar of gunfire, the whistle of shells. Faces of men I could not save flash like lightning. I swallow hard.

"They are all gone. I am still here. That should not be possible."

One of the photographers moves closer, and flash after flash hits me like detonations. I can feel my heartbeat in my throat. My chest wants to tighten further, to shut down, to disappear. But I force myself upright and imagine the names of those who did not make it.

"Every flash is a memory. Every smile is borrowed."

A general comes from somewhere with a clap on my

back, with a hand heavy with expectation. I hear words from him that I do not register, phrases about courage and sacrifice. My jaw aches from holding the smile, my lips feel stiff, brittle, like parchment.

My wife leans closer, whispering something I cannot hear over the noise. While my children look up at me, with eyes filled with trust and pride. The desire to protect them is the only thing that keeps me anchored in this room, not the noise, not the lights, not the cameras.

"Do not let them see. Do not let them know. Not now."

A reporter waves a microphone. "Colonel, what does this medal mean to you?"

I force the words out, "It is an honor. I am grateful to serve." The words feel empty in my mouth, hollow echoes of what I am supposed to say.

"Grateful? To whom? To the men who lie in the dirt? To the families I left behind in the desert?"

Another flash goes off. My eyes close for a fraction of a second. It is enough to see it again. The fire, the blood, the smoke curling into the sky like black ribbons. I could hear the screams. The orders. The fear in the voices.

"Control it. You cannot break here. Not in front of them."

I open my eyes. The crowd has not noticed. They only see the hero, the medal, the pride of their country. I squeeze my wife's hand. Not for reassurance, but for survival.

"Keep it together. One more step. One more handshake."

Another Handshake, another pat on the back. All of this lands in my skull like a gunshot. I remember lying awake while the world slept, counting bodies, counting breaths, counting what I failed to save.

"You are supposed to be proud. You are supposed to be happy. But how?"

A young officer looks up to me, eyes bright with admiration. He is ready to take the same path I have walked, ready to believe in medals and honor. I want to warn him, to scream, but the words do not come out. I cannot break the illusion.

"Do not speak. Do not break him. He will find out soon enough."

The applause comes again in waves. I bow slightly, a gesture of courtesy, and feel the weight of the medal like a chain around my chest. The media, the crowd, even my family believe the façade. I smile for them but inside I am hollow.

"I am a ghost. They are cheering for a ghost."

My daughter tugs at my sleeve. Her presence gives me strength, enough to keep me sane and hide my true self.

"Do not let them know. Not here. Not ever."

I smile, shake more hands, answer questions with words that do not touch the truth. I leave no room for doubt in their eyes. I give them the hero. I give them the story they want to believe.

The war inside stays buried beneath the medal, beneath the applause, and my mind counts every echo of it.

The claps will end. The crowd will fade. And I would still be here, smiling, carrying it all.

"Smile. Breathe. Stand. They cannot see. They cannot know."

The applause finally thins, but the energy in the room lingers, a residue that clings to my skin. People begin to step aside, move toward cocktails and congratulations. I follow them, walking only on instinct, not because I want to. Every step feels heavy, weighted by the medal, by the memories, by the lie I must carry.

"Keep moving. Do not stop. Do not fall apart."

I catch glimpses of journalists scribbling, microphones still poised. Their questions hover in the air like smoke, waiting for an answer. I smile and stop for a minute to answer briefly. Each word tastes hollow, like ash on my tongue.

"My words mean nothing. They only want the story, not the man behind it."

My wife gently guides me toward the back of the room where the air is quieter, the chandeliers farther above, the sound of clapping just a distant echo. She does not speak, only squeezes my hand. Our children follow with small footsteps.

I could finally breathe, far from those light, those eyes. My knees feel weak like noodles. As I close my eyes for a second, the memories come in fragments, uninvited. The night sky ripped apart by tracer fire. Men screaming my name for instructions. The smell of burning metals and bodies. I could hear my own breathing in the middle of it, ragged and desperate.

"Why am I still here? Why am I still breathing when they are not?"

I feel my wife's hand on my shoulder. She does not ask, does not look away. She just stays. My daughter's small hand touches my sleeve. My son leans into my side. Their presence is real, but it cannot reach the pieces of me scattered across deserts and streets, buried in ruins.

"I am supposed to be here. I am supposed to smile. But none of this belongs to me."

I look down at the medal. Silver. Shiny. Perfect. Cold.

Everyone will remember this day, frame it, tell the story of the decorated hero. But no one will see what it costs. No one will see the body scared with memories, the mind full of explosions and grief, the heart heavy with guilt.

"Behind this metal, behind this uniform, I am just a man who survived. That is all."

I glance around only to see the room bubbling with conversations and smiling faces. I smile back, to give them what they came for: the hero, the story, the photograph.

"My smile is not mine. It belongs to them, to their applause, to their cameras. It is a mask. A Perfect mask."

I bend down to pick up my daughter, and she hugs me tight. Her hair smells like home, like safe afternoons, like a scent of safety. I close my eyes against the flash of memory, hold her close, and let the medal press into my chest. My son steps forward and clasps my hand. The weight of their trust presses against me in a way heavier than the medal.

"Do not let the truth show."

I lift my head and step back into the light. Another photographer moves in, capturing this perfect image: the father, the hero, the family man. I pose for them, while also fighting a war which never ends. Inside my mind, the screams don't stop, I cannot escape the flashes of heaps of bodies.

And yet I walk through the room as if I do, shaking hands, nodding, smiling, every movement a calculated echo of the man they want me to be. My family is near enough to tether me to the present, but I know when I step outside, when the applause fades completely, the smile will stop and I will be alone with the memories.

I glance once more at the medal, let the silver catch the light. It is heavy and shining. A say it is a symbol of bravery. But for me, it is proof that I am here, that I survived, that I will continue to survive, even if the world cannot see the cost.

I pull my family close and step back into the room. The applauses will rise again for someone else, somewhere else. But today it is my turn to wear the mask.

"Keep moving. Keep surviving. Behind the smile, I am still here."

****

STORY 5

Lipstick in Red Light

She pressed the lipstick to her lips, painting them blood red with quiet precision. She paused, letting the color settle, then leaned slightly closer to the cracked mirror that hung crookedly on the wall. The reflection showed her middle-aged face, the faint lines of years lived etched around her eyes and the bright smear of color standing out like a warning.

She felt the smooth glide still lingering on her mouth and let her mind drift. Each line of color was a reminder that she still existed, that she still had choices, however small. In this room, where walls seemed to breathe with fear and whispered secrets, the red on her lips was a declaration: she could not be erased, even if the world tried.

Around her, the air was thick with the mingled scents of cheap perfume and sweat. The faint hum of the city outside barely reached the room, but inside, the low murmur of other women and the scrape of worn heels against the concrete floor created an uneasy rhythm. Each sound was a marker of presence, a reminder that she was not alone, even here.

Her mind wandered back on its own. She remembered the man she had trusted, the one who had promised her love, who had spoken in whispers of forever and held her hand as if the world belonged only to them. She had believed him completely, imagining a life they would have built together. And then the truth hit, sharp and brutal. He had delivered her into this life, sold her with the same hands that had once caressed her. Each memory pressed against her chest like a physical ache as she pressed her lips together, letting the lipstick seal them in defiance.

In the corner of the room, she saw a new arrival. The young girl stumbled, hands clutching at the folds of her dress, eyes wide and shimmering with terror. She avoided any eye contact as if the walls themselves could swallow her whole. The older woman knew all these reactions well as they mirrored her own fear when she had first arrived, raw and unshaped.

The girl's lips quivered in fear. Her skin glowed with the freshness of innocence and new life. She had come from somewhere else, a different home perhaps. The older woman could almost see the betrayal pressing down on her though she did not yet know it. She had been that girl once, clinging to hope even as it was stripped away piece by piece.

Her eyes darted to corners, to other women, to imagined exits. Her feet scraped softly against the floor. Fear radiated from her in waves. The older woman had been her once. She had known that same terror and betrayal, the same disbelief and confusion. She had curled into corners and learned survival slowly and painfully. She knew this girl would learn too, one day, stroke by stroke, habit by habit.

The woman picked up the lipstick again and pressed it to her lips, letting the blood red sink into her skin, a counterweight to fear. Each stroke was deliberate, a meditation, a way to claim herself in a world that tried to erase her. She felt the faint scratch of the tip against her mouth, the soft waxiness, the slight stick as it set. She inhaled deeply, the color itself settling in her mind like a steady rhythm she could hold on to.

Outside, the city murmured in the distance, a sound that felt almost irrelevant. Inside, the hum of the room carried on. Time in this place moved differently. It was not measured by clocks but by rituals and small repetitions. Each stroke of lipstick was a meditation, each glance, each breath, each silent calculation a survival technique. She observed the room, memorized patterns and listened to the shuffle of skirts. Each sound and motion was a code, a map of this confined universe, and she learned it, remembered it, and let it guide her.

She remembered how the world had once measured her, when youth had been everything. Bright eyes, smooth skin, those had been her only currency. Years had since written themselves into her body, lines across her face, scars beneath her clothes, aches that never left. Men came to her less often now, and when they did, it was with a different hunger, one that sought not beauty but something cheaper, more desperate. In their eyes she was no longer a woman, only an object.

A soft whimper pulled her back. The older woman looked at the young girl with a mixture of pity and resignation. She wanted to whisper truths into her ear, to warn her how the nights would grind her down, how mirrors would turn into enemies, how the smell of perfume and sweat would cling until she forgot her own scent. But words could never prepare her. Pain would. Pain was the only teacher here, and repetition its lesson.

The room carried its own symphony. Laughter rang out sharp and brittle, cracking before it could sound real. Whispered secrets darted between women and then vanished. The walls held the smell of incense mixed with cigarettes, and the bitter tang of sweat and alcohol.

The door creaked open and the room fell still. A man stepped inside, his boots struck the floor with a slow, deliberate weight, his eyes sharp and unfeeling as he scanned the room, then fixed his gaze on the older woman.

"Ready the young blood," he commanded with an unyielding voice, jerking his chin toward the shivering girl. "And when you are done," he added, "put some lipstick on her."

****

CHAPTER 6

The Night of the Unspoken Battles

The key turned in the lock with a soft click, and the door gave way beneath a steady hand. A hollow creak followed as it swung inward, the sound carrying through the narrow apartment like an unwelcome announcement. The air smelled faintly of dust and old paint, as though the rooms had been holding their breath all day. He stepped inside, shoulders bowed, his frame carrying the invisible weight of another day that had taken more than it gave.

He reached for the switch, and a pale light spilled across the room, revealing a space that looked more like an abandoned shelter than a home.

The silence was suffocating.

He set his laptop bag down on the table without care, the thud louder than it should have been in such stillness. His shoulders slumped, his tie hung loose, and his shoes dragged against the floor as he made his way to the bed. He collapsed onto it, the springs groaning under his weight. The ceiling stared back at him blankly, its white dulled with stains of time.

"What am I even doing," he whispered.
The question had no answer. It never did.

He was thirty-two, and what did he have? Long hours bent over a desk, words from a boss that carried more sting than recognition, a string of deadlines that dissolved as soon as they were met. He could not remember the last time he had smiled without forcing it, or the last time his body had not carried exhaustion like a permanent layer.

Every day was the same. Hustle of the morning

trains, office corridors heavy with the smell of coffee and sweat, the voice of a boss who spoke in clipped orders, deadlines that had no end. He worked, he nodded, he bent himself to fit whatever was asked, and then he returned here, to this hollow room which he called home.

He pressed his palms against his eyes, as if to block the world out.

Then old memories of her surfaced, sharp and unwelcome. He had always been buried in work, and she had wanted only the glitter, the weekend dinners, the photogenic scenes, the fleeting attention he could spare. After seven years together, she let go when reality pressed in. Today he had heard of her wedding, the proof that she had moved on, and he had never been part of it.

Is this all I was born for. To shuffle papers, to nod at people I do not respect, to watch years roll by until nothing is left of me.

The weight of thirty-two years pressed on him like a stone. He felt older than he was, worn by repetition, carved down by demands that never relented. Others seemed to be living, laughing, chasing something. He was only enduring.

He stared at the ceiling until his eyes burned. A hollow thought crept in, one that had made its way into his nights more often than he wanted to admit. *What if it all just stopped?* The notion of silence deeper than this room, a rest that was final, tugged at him. His mind flickered through the possibilities in sharp images: pills scattered across the floor, a rope, a blade. Each came with a strange detachment, as though he were watching someone else consider them.

But another thought intruded, heavier than the first. *What about the loans?* He could see the numbers etched into his mind, the balance that had followed him like a shadow. If he were gone, the weight would not vanish; it would fall on the shoulders of the two people who had carried him since the day he was born. The thought of them bent under the weight of his debts, explaining to bank officials, scraping together their savings, broke something inside him. He could never do that to them.

They had given him everything. More than he ever deserved. His chest tightened. He reached for his phone and opened the photograph of them he always carried. His parents stared back from the picture, younger then, stronger, their smiles unguarded. He studied their faces as if memorizing them anew. He remembered the last time he had visited his parents, his father's hair had thinned, how his mother's hands trembled when she poured tea.

They had given everything so he could stand where he was. His father rising before dawn to work long hours, his mother stretching meals so there was always enough, both of them silencing their own needs so his could be met. He remembered childhood mornings when his father's hand rested briefly on his head before leaving, the smell of soap lingering after. He remembered evenings when his mother stitched clothes by weak light, humming softly though her back must have ached.

They had carried so much, weathered so much, always making room for him in their world. He could not repay them for the sacrifices hidden in those lines. They had supported him through every failure, every late night, every moment when he could not stand on his own.

And what had he given them in return. A son who came home each night too tired to call, too drained to visit. A son who could barely hold himself together. He blinked and felt the burn in his eyes.

He rolled onto his side and stared at the darkened wall.

Tears prickled at his eyes, though they did not fall. He pressed the photo to his chest, as though it could shield him from the tide of his thoughts. His breathing slowed, his body giving in to the heaviness.

He had not known when sleep had finally claimed him, his mind still lingering on his parents and all they had carried for him. Morning arrived in a blur. The shrill sound cut through the fog of his mind. He groped for the phone, eyes half open. Eight. The screen glared at him. He realized he was late for the office.

He stumbled from the bed, pulling on a shirt, buttoning it unevenly, splashing water on his face until it ran down his collar. He picked up his laptop bag from the dusty table and hurriedly tied his shoes clumsily.

He opened the door, ready to rush into another day, when the sound of voices reached him.

The corridor was crowded. His neighbors stood clustered near the apartment next to his, their faces drawn while murmuring slowly. The air was charged and intense, as if the walls themselves were holding a secret.

He approached cautiously, his stomach knotting with unease. One of the neighbors he knew only in passing stood near the doorway.

The man turned, his face grave.

"The one who lived here," he said softly, nodding toward the closed door. "He took his life last night. Too much pressure from work, they say."

The young man stood frozen, staring at the door of the neighboring flat.

****

STORY 7

Till the Last Flame Lasts

The lighter coughed a spark and the flame rose, trembling in the cell's shadows. I cupped it between my fingers and brought it to the tip of the cigarette. The tobacco hissed, a tiny protest in the quiet, and I drew the smoke into my lungs, letting it burn through the hollow places that sorrow and fear had carved into me over months of confinement. The ember glowed faintly, fragile as a heartbeat, yet it was enough to remind me that I was still alive, even if life itself had long abandoned me.

The concrete walls leaned in around me, rough to the touch, sweating with years of water that had seeped through hairline cracks. The iron bars bore rust in stubborn patches, flaking like old skin, and the cot beneath me sagged under the memory of every prisoner who had come before. The single bulb above buzzed and flickered, but its feeble light was powerless to stop the shadows waiting to crawl in.

I drew in another puff, letting the smoke fill my chest, seep into the crevices of my lungs, wrap around my thoughts.

It was bitter.

Bitter like every word I had spoken that no one had heard. Bitter like the weight of signatures pressed against me in court, like the weight of the courtroom, like the calm voice of my friend that had sentenced me with one pointed declaration. The scenes replayed over and over, slicing into my memory like a knife.

The Honourable Minister. I saw him, sitting at the back of the courtroom in silk shirts and polished shoes, untouched by the lives he had crushed under paper and pen. He had the world at his feet while I became a shadow in a room I could not escape. Smoke curled and twisted in the dim light as I let my mind drift back to the square.

Dust swirled beneath our boots, banners lifted like fragile suns, hands shaking not from fear but from hope. Red and black paint smeared across the stone, banners declaring, "This land is ours," trembling in the wind, trembling with us. I could feel the wetness of paint under my fingers, the grit of dust pressed into skin, the pull of adrenaline in our muscles. Some of us feared the Minister's men. Others feared only silence. I had believed then, with all the reckless certainty of youth, that together we could bend the world. I had believed truth carried weight.

But the world turned its back on truth, and came the guns.

Uniformed men firing into the air, bullets ripping through the crowd as screams tore across every corner, filling every lung and ear. Children fell. Voices that had called for hope turned to terror and were swallowed in the smoke and chaos. Somewhere inside it, voices accused me of starting it, that I had called for violence, that I had thrown the first stone, that I had been the instigator.

Lies. Lies. Lies.

I had not moved against anyone. I had only shouted words that dissolved into the roar of destruction. Yet the world, as always, listened to those who had polished shoes and silk shirts, not to the ones who bled in the square.

Betrayal cut next, sharper than any knife.

He was my friend. The one who had marched beside me, painted slogans beside me and held the line beside me. Now, calm and rehearsed, pointing at me in court. Words fell from his lips like stones, every syllable designed to shatter my existence. Coin, fear, promises, something I could not name had turned him against me.

I drew another drag, searching for warmth, for solace. But nothing soothed the wounds. Nothing lightened the load. The walls leaned closer, as if ready to listen my story. The air hissed through cracks in the concrete, carrying whispers that only I could hear. Every footstep in the hall outside, every clank of metal against metal, sounded like a summons, like the world itself reminding me of what had been closing in for months, for years.

The trial appeared again in my mind. The Minister smiling at the back row, untouched by anything, his polished hands resting lightly, the judge nodding and passing judgment without even listening, the reporters writing lies as if they had read the script before the words were spoken. The law had been a theatre. I was the one actor who refused to perform his role.

Smoke filled my lungs, filled the hollow of my chest, settled in the empty spaces that hope and trust had left behind. I wondered if anyone would remember me. Not the headlines, not the trial, not the accusations. Would anyone remember that I had stood in the square with empty hands, shouting for truth, that I had never struck? Could smoke carry memory beyond these walls, into a world that had so quickly forgotten me?

Hunger clawed at my belly. My stomach protested, twisting into knots, yet I ignored it. Food was irrelevant here. My body had been trained for stillness, for absence, for the inevitable end. Smoke was my sustenance, filling every corner of the cell, every hollow of my lungs, every crack in my mind. I let it coat my tongue, bitter and sharp, like betrayal, like fire, like the Minister's calm, polished smile.

I drew again, long, deep, letting the smoke reach my bones. I imagined it carrying all of my despair, my memory, my hopes. The thought of eternal darkness leaned closer, but I did not flinch. I had faced the square, the guns, the screams. I had faced the betrayal. I could face this too.

I pressed my hand against the wall, feeling the rough concrete biting into my skin. I felt the tiny grooves and pits, traced the cracks that had multiplied over decades. I held the ember tighter, a fragile sun marking the slow passage of time, a reminder that I still existed even as the world erased me.

Another drag, longer this time, slow and deliberate. Perhaps my words would fade, my voice swallowed, but my memory would linger in smoke, in thought, in the ember that refused to die until the last second.

I drew another drag, my throat burned, but I welcomed it. Pain was honest. Unlike the world, unlike the Minister, unlike the friend who had betrayed me for reasons too petty and cruel to name, the smoke did not lie.

I remembered the square again. I had believed then that I could bend the world. I had believed truth carried weight. But truth, I realized, had always been lighter than the men who wielded power, duller than the lies that fell from polished lips, and more fragile than the human heart.

I could see the faces of my fallen comrades in the square, children, the mothers, the fathers, the hands reaching for banners that had never carried enough weight. I wondered, bitterly, if the world would ever know my truth. Would anyone remember the man who had stood for justice. The soul which had been crushed by the machinery of power and fear?

Another drag. I held the smoke in this time. My thoughts spiralled. Could the final breath of a man condemned whisper to the world a truth it refused to see in life? I imagined the wind carrying the smoke beyond the walls, beyond the city, beyond the reach of men in silk shirts and polished shoes, to ears willing to remember.

The ember shrank, smaller now, trembling in my fingers like a dying star. I cupped it as if it contained everything I had left. I inhaled deeply one last time, letting it mark me, letting it burn through me. The taste was honest. The smoke curled upward, curling into the shadows, as if reaching toward a world that had long ago turned its back.

I could hear the corridor outside now, heavy footsteps approaching, the click of the lock turning, the bars rattling. The guard's voice, calm and final, called my name. The preparation was finished. The path to the execution room awaited, and I knew with the certainty that had grown in these months of confinement that there would be no turning back.

I stood and walked to the door with stiff legs. The ember of the cigarette had shrunk to a final point, glowing with the last measure of life I could claim. I held it a moment longer, as if I could impress upon it the weight of my memory, the injustice of the world, the betrayal, the innocence that had been swallowed by lies. Then, I let it fade, the last trace of fire vanishing into ash between my fingers.

The guard opened the cell. And the light spilled in from the corridor, in a hurry to reclaim whatever was left into my cell. I stepped forward, letting the ash slip from my fingers. I did not look at him. I did not need to. The sound of his boots on the stone floor, the click of metal handcuffs, was enough. I was ready.

As I walked toward the inevitability, my mind

wandered one final time. Perhaps someone, someday, would remember me. Perhaps the truth of my innocence would someday come out and outshine the Minister's polished smile. Perhaps smoke of my cigarette would carry my story beyond the walls, beyond the world, into a place where justice, delayed by centuries, could still matter.

And then the corridor ended. The last shadow fell behind me giving way to a room full of the brightest lights, waiting for my embrace. The guard placed a hand on my shoulder, reminding me to hurry up.

I did not resist. I stepped forward in the execution chamber. I carried with me the slow burn of all that had been lost, and the stubborn, fragile insistence that even if the world forgot, I had held on to morals until the last flame lasted.

Author's Note

The Echoes of the Silent Heart is not a collection born of lightness but of shadows. These stories come from the fragile spaces where love and grief meet, where survival carries scars, and where silence can weigh heavier than words.

Each piece reflects the quiet burdens we carry, the wounds that do not vanish, the fears that return in stillness, and the moments of tenderness that flicker even in despair. They are reminders that beneath the surface of every life lies a struggle often unseen, a loneliness that asks to be recognized.

Together, these stories form a portrait of human vulnerability, showing how memory clings, how intimacy can be both salvation and ache, and how the search for meaning persists even in the darkest nights.

This book is for those who know that sadness lingers long after the world has moved on and who understand that sometimes the deepest echoes are the ones we cannot silence.

www.ingramcontent.com/pod-product-compliance
Ingram Content Group UK Ltd.
Pitfield, Milton Keynes, MK11 3LW, UK
UKHW021410190726
13845UKWH00028B/999

9 789334 426458